The Animals' Environmental Protest

Chesney Orme

Published by New Generation Publishing in 2021

Copyright © Chesney Orme 2021

First Edition

Paperback ISBN: 978-1-80369-118-3
Hardback ISBN: 978-1-80369-119-0

www.newgeneration-publishing.com

New Generation Publishing

I dedicate this book to Billie Rowena the youngest member to join my family. Born on December 16th 2020, who hopefully will grow up with her generation in a better and more caring world.

ACKNOWLEDGEMENTS

To my family and friends who have helped and inspired me to write this book which will hopefully highlight the chaos and suffering we humans are inflicting on our treasured animals due to our laziness and selfish behaviour towards them who we live alongside on our planet Earth.

My thanks to the following for their support: -
my sister Sarah, Lucy, Carole and her children Leo and Molly. Lauren, Paul and Billie.
James and Emily.
Eric Johnson for introducing me to the wise old owl.
Les Taylor for taking fantastic care in looking after Scrappy the cat mentioned in the book. Scrappy was abandoned and left on a motorway as a kitten and was rescued by two kind scrap men.
Sally and Isabel for their contribution.
Nick Roberts the illustrator for doing such a wonderful job and has been a pleasure to work with.
And most specially I would like to say thank you to my girlfriend Jacky for all her support and encouragement to finish the story and have my book published.

This is the story of our woodland creatures and their mission to communicate with the two leggers and change forever the impact of litter in the environment they all share.

The story of our woodland creatures and their mission to communicate with the two leggers and change forever the impact of litter in the environment they all share.

The hedgehog family, Mr. and Mrs. Spike, and their children, Harriet and Harry were talking about all the bad things happening to their world.

"What's all this stuff blowing everywhere?" asked Harry.

"I overheard these two leggers call it plastic waste," replied Harriet. "Do you know, they refer to us as animals, even though they are the primitive ones! We've been here for thousands of years longer than they have. The world was never this messy until they came."

"I've heard they can fly to the moon and back, yet they can't keep their only world tidy."

"I agree, but we can't communicate with these two-legged litter bugs, so we need to figure a way for them to stop damaging our species!"

Harry turns toward Harriet and says, "I've got an idea! Roll over on that crisp packet on your spikes, lie in the road and then start walking." Harriet gives him a confused glance. Harry continues to explain, "I know it's dangerous, but you've got to get their attention. I will stand the other side of the road and tell you when to cross."

"Do you think I'm stupid? These two leggers in their noisy machines will just think I'm a crisp packet, give me no respect and run over me. Then you would lose your only sister! How would you feel if that happened?"

"Okay, bad idea. Well, how about you put the crisp packet on your spikes and zigzag across the pavement? That will get their attention, hopefully they won't tread on you," said Harry.

"That's not so smart either, someone might just step on me and throw me in the bin. Then I'm dead anyway!" replied Harriet.

"So how can we campaign? We need to create a plan and work together to try and save as many animals as possible from this horrible mess the two leggers have got us into."

"How do we start?" asked Harriet.

"Step one," said Harry, "ask Mum and Dad."

When the two little hedgehogs finally find their

parents, the whole family sit under the rhododendron bush, where they often went for shelter when it rained.

"Where has all this plastic waste come from?" asked Harriet.

"It all started years ago. When I was your age and lived with Grandma and Grandad, the fields and villages were free from all this rubbish and waste," explained Mum.

"So how did it end up like this?" said Harriet.

Mr. Spike sat down next to his family and continued to explain.

"In those days there was no plastic blowing around, just the odd paper bag which would usually end up getting stuck in a tree or a bush. After a few days, if it rained, the bag would just break down and dissolve into the ground because, paper is made from trees which makes it a natural material! Tin cans and glass bottles would be collected and recycled by the two leggers. I saw them take them back to the shops, then a few moments later coming out, with them full again." Mrs. Spike nodded in agreement.

"The towns and countryside were lovely places to live. Not like today, somehow the two leggers have changed the packaging material to something else called 'plastic'. Plastic isn't a natural material, and it doesn't break down so instead it interferes with nature. It can make animals very ill if they eat it.

"One day when I was walking along with your dad,

we saw a cat with its head stuck in a tin can, it must've been looking for food, poor thing."

"It was there for days; we couldn't help it," said Mr. Spike.

"What happened to it?" asked Harry.

"Luckily for the cat, one of the two leggers pulled its head out and saved its life! Some of them are kind and thoughtful towards nature and animals whereas most need educating about all the harmful things, they are doing to ruin the world," replied Mr. Spike.

"So, what can we do to educate them so they learn what is needed to be more careful, because it's not like we can just talk to them?" said Harry.

Little did they know, Mr. Twit the wise old owl was listening in on their conversation. Mr. Twit had heard everything that the family had been talking about. He carefully hopped down from his branch and walked towards the bush.

"Hello! My name is Mr. Twit, but you can call me Twit. Sorry that I was being nosy, but I think I may have a way to communicate with the two leggers."

"What do you think we should do?" asked Harriet intriguingly.

"We need to get all the animals together and arrange a meeting around here. I can arrange it tonight when they return for their tea. I will explain to them what we have been talking about," said Twit.

"What a great idea!" said Mum.

"I'll fly back tomorrow, same place, same time and tell you what they have to say. See you tomorrow!" and Twit flew back to his tree. The hedgehogs all waved goodbye and went back to their foraging; they had got a long night ahead and a daytime sleep before for tomorrow teatime came along. Harriet and Harry were excited as they'd never been to a meeting before with all the different animals.

Teatime came early this summer evening around 5 o'clock. Harriet and Harry were already up discussing their plans and what they were going to say at the meeting. They were really excited about being able to help clean up their countryside.

Mr. and Mrs. Spike woke up and saw Harriet and Harry tidying up the leaves. Mrs. Spike shouted "What are you doing? You need to eat something and then you can wait for Mr. Twit to arrive." After a long wait, Harry and Harriet were getting bored; they had forgotten that Mr. Twit stays up all night too because he is nocturnal.

It was getting late when suddenly they heard a very noisy twit coming into land. He skidded through the leaves with his talons outstretched. Harry and Harriet turned around in excitement.

"Come on, Twit! Tell us the news, have we got a meeting?" asked Harry.

"Slow down," said Twit. "I've just flown miles to get here, let me get my breath back."

Mum and Dad appeared out from under the leaves to greet him. "Hello, Twit," said Mr. and Mrs. Spike. "Have you got news for us?" "Yes, brilliant news," replied Twit. "The entire woodland is enthusiastic about your idea to get together and discuss how we can teach the two leggers to be more responsible for their waste materials. This is brilliant! Everyone is very excited, the meeting is on Saturday, near the top of the waterfall."

Harriet and Harry thought that would be a great idea. "If it's a hot day, we could go for a dip and we don't have to go far for a drink."

"As chairman, I will introduce you all," said Twit; he then read out a list of all the woodland creatures who would be attending.

- Bill the Badger
- Sly the fox
- Joe the crow
- Snowy the rabbit
- Snid the grass snake
- Ben the sheepdog, from Berristall Hall Farm
- Willy the woodpecker
- Jug the hare
- Scratty the wood pigeon
- Goofy the beaver
- Rodney the water rat
- Milly the mole
- Spotty the deer
- Nutty the squirrel
- Loner the goose
- Trap the mouse

And many more..."

"What about me?" said Maurice the cat, who was listening in. "I'm the one who got the tin can stuck on my head! And one of the two leggers helped me get it off, it was very kind. I need to be there too".

"Right, everyone I will see you all on Saturday around midday get your thoughts together and think about what you are going to say – see you then, bye."

"Bye, bye!" shouted the hedgehogs, as they watched Twit take off into the late afternoon sun.

"He is very well-organized," said Mrs. Spike.

"Yes," said Mr. Spike, "that is why he's called a wise old owl."

"I'm really looking forward to Saturday," said Harriet. "Should we take a packed lunch, or can we just forage around in the wood, Mum?"

"No, there will be plenty to eat near the waterfall," said Mum, "and we will make sure we all have a good breakfast before we leave."

"Can we go to sleep now until Saturday?" said Harry, "Then it will come round quicker."

"No, that's not a good idea," said Harriet. "We have got to think about what we're going to say when it's our turn to speak Harry." "Oh, I never thought about that."

"Right, you two go off into the woods, talk to each other and rehearse what you are going to speak about," said Mum and Dad, "and we will do the same."

So off to the woods scurried Harry and Harriet and

looked for a good hiding place to sit and talk. They came across a big oak tree, with a massive hole in the bottom where the tree had gone rotten with age. "Look, Harry, this is a great hiding place for us."

"Brilliant," said Harry, "we could make this our permanent den." They both peeped in cautiously, to make absolutely sure no one else had got there first, then crept in quietly following a sunbeam of natural light streaming through the treetops illuminating the middle of the tree.

"This is fantastic," said Harriet. "I wish we had found this den before." They both sat down and started to rehearse what they were going to say at the meeting and came up with all sorts of ideas.

The time passed quickly they were enjoying themselves, then gradually the light faded as the sun was setting. It began to go dark inside the tree, so they decided to make their way back home through the woods. The twilight was lighting up the forest floor in beautiful patterns, as the light penetrated through the canopy of branches which covered the treetops.
At last, they were back with Mum and Dad in the safety of their home.
Mum asked, "Have you managed to pull your speech together yet?"
"Yes," they both replied.
"Well go on then, tell us what you are going to say," said Dad.
"No," they both said, "it is a secret. You will have to wait until Saturday. We don't want you pinching our ideas."
"What about you?" asked Harry.
"Have you got your speech ready, Dad?"
"Yes," he said abruptly. "Same applies, you will have to wait till Saturday and see."
"I can't wait until Saturday," said Harriet. "I've never made a speech before or met any of the other animals together in one place."
"Me neither," said Harry.

"Isn't it exciting, Harriet? We don't know what we have started."

"I hope there's no falling out between any of them," said Harriet. "You know some of them don't get on very well."

"I don't think we will have any problem with Twit running the show," said Harry. "He'll just swoop down and let them know they are not welcome if they can't behave. You know how strict he is. They are all a bit scared of Twit, they have seen him in action before."

It's now Friday night. Mum shouts "Come on, it's time for bed, you know we have a very important day tomorrow." "Come on, Harriet," said Harry, "let's see which one can get to sleep first." They both closed their eyes and within minutes they were in the Land of Nod.

Saturday morning arrived, it was 5 a.m. It was just becoming daylight and the early morning sun was shining through the gaps between the leaves on the bush that Harry and Harriet were asleep under.

First to wake up is Harry. He stretched out his little
legs and did a big yawn then he suddenly realized
it's Saturday. He jumps up and down with excitement
and can't wait to wake Harriet up, who was still fast
asleep. He pokes her, then rocks her.
She says, 'Harry, it's the middle of the night, go back
to sleep. Harry persists,
"But it's Saturday."
"I know it's Saturday, but I want to have some more
sleep. If you don't go back to sleep, you won't be fit
for the meeting you will fall asleep and miss it all."
"OK," said Harry, "I will try." He curled up again and
closed his eyes and managed to go back to sleep.
Next thing it was 8 a.m. Mum and Dad called "Out,
come on you two, it's time to get going." They both
got up a bit blurry-eyed and crawled out from under
the leaves.
"Now get some breakfast and get ready to go, we've
got a long walk to the waterfall and it's going to be a
hot day!" Mum shouts. "It's getting on, it's now 9 a.m.
We don't want to be late. You started this, it would
not look very good if we were the last to arrive."

"Right, we're off," said Spike, "don't go running
away, we don't want to lose you."
"Do you know how to get there?" asked Mum. "Not
really," said Harry.
"Well then, stay close to us. If you get lost, follow
the sun as we are going south."

Suddenly Harriet tripped up and rolled in a ball right down the embankment.

Harry shouts "Are you OK, Harriet?"

"No," she replied.

"Wait there, Dad is coming, stay still Harriet, I'm coming down. Dad climbs down the embankment carefully, as it is very steep and dangerous. He gets to Harriet and asked what happened.

"I tripped over and got tangled up in those plastic rings, then fell down the banking."

"Stay still," said Dad, "and I'll try to get you untangled. These are very strong plastic rings," he said. "I've seen these two leggers carrying cans in them when they picnic in the woods. This is exactly why we need this meeting. Keep still, I have you untangled now."

"Are you OK now, Harriet?"

"Yes, thanks, Dad."

"Are you sure you're OK and fit to carry on?" asked

Mum. "Or shall we go home?"

"No, no, no," said Harriet. "I'm not really hurt," and they climbed back up the banking back on to the path where Mum and Harry were waiting eagerly for them to get to the top.

Mum gave Harriet a big reassuring hug and said, "Right, now stay by my side the rest of the way. We don't want any more accidents."

"We should bring these plastic rings along with us," said Dad, "and show everyone how dangerous they are."

"Good idea," says Mum, "but get a move on that's lost us half an hour. Good job we set off early."

The morning was warming up, so they try to keep in the shady part of the trees. Then all of a sudden they heared a bumping and thundering noise coming from behind them. They stopped for a moment and suddenly a badger appeared, a bit out of breath, and ran straight passed them. That must be Bill the badger, he's on his way to the meeting, remember Twit told us he has asked him to come;

"Oh good," said Dad, "at least we've got one animal turning up. It's a start."

"How far is it now, Dad?' asked Harry.

"Mm I think we're over halfway there, won't be long now. Look quick, Mum, look up there, that's Twit waving at us and pointing the way with his wing. He is busy flying around making sure no one is lost."

"I think you are right," said Mum.

Just then they see a deer leaping up and down, travelling very fast through the woods. "That must be Spotty. She is another one Twit has invited."

"Why is she called Spotty?" asked Harriet.

"Because she has got spots, silly," said Harry.

"Go on then, smarty pants," said Dad. "What sort of deer is she then?"

"I don't know," said Harry.

"Well don't be so rude to your sister. She is a fallow deer. Right be careful now," said Dad, "we're getting close to the stream's edge. We will follow the stream right up to the waterfall, it won't be long now."

"Look, Mum, there's Rodney the water rat, we must be getting close, look again over there it's Loner the goose and Goofy the beaver going up the stream. I am getting really excited now," said Harriet.

"Look up, the birds are flying above us. And look over there's, it's Nutty the squirrel leaping from branch to branch, he's got something on his back," said Harry. "I suppose it could be his packed lunch."

"Look all of you up the stream is that the waterfall?" "Yes", said Dad, "we are just a few minutes away, we can slow down now, we have plenty of time." The noise from the waterfall was getting louder and louder, as they get closer.

"That's not a good place for a meeting," said Mum. "We won't be able to hear ourselves speak."

Just as they approach, they see Ben the sheep dog from Berristall Hall Farm running back and forth, rounding all the animals together guiding them to the far right where

there is a large stone circle away from the noise of the waterfall.

"This has been a meeting place for thousands of years. What a fantastic place," said Spike. "Twit certainly knows how to organize everyone. That's why he is called a wise old owl."

All the animals are now guided around the circle by Ben the sheep dog and the stones in the circle are filling up quickly as the animals turn up. They are all a bit quiet and seem a bit nervous as more and more of them turn up and stand behind. The circle is now packed and the trees around are full of birds. Word has surely got around the woods.

Twit perches on a large stone about 6 metres above the circle at about 12 o'clock, if you imagine your watch being the circle.

"Good afternoon everybody, it's nice to see such a great turnout for such an important event, especially to those who are normally asleep during the day. I will start by introducing myself, I am Mr Twit. You can call me Twit. I would like to thank all those invited who have come along today in support of our campaign on plastic pollution and general rubbish left by these two leggers in our treasured countryside, rivers and woodland. Before we start this meeting, I would like to say a few words to all:
No falling out
No fighting
Make friends

And get to know each other and share your stories on this issue of rubbish spoiling where we all live. And just one last word to Mr Fox.

Sly, I know you very well, but today all these animals are your friends not your dinner, so stop licking your lips and concentrate on what's going on, or you'll have me to contend with as you know, you don't like that, from past experiences. Right, let's get down to business."

All quiet then, we can start." Everyone goes very quiet, then there's a loud grunting noise – It's Smelly the pig from the Farm. He's late. "Why didn't you ask me?" said Smelly.

Twit replied, "Sorry Smelly, I couldn't get round to ask everyone, but you are very welcome to join the rest of the guests."

"I must tell you," said Smelly, "I can eat most things, but I can't eat this plastic rubbish, it blows everywhere and ends up in my food." "OK," said Twit, "you'll have your say later. Let's move on. First, I would like to open this meeting by asking the Spike family to explain why they have asked me to call this meeting."

"Well, good afternoon everybody. I'm pleased to

see such a fantastic turn out. Today let's hope we can make a big change in these two leggers' attitude to rubbish and stop them littering up our environment. I would firstly like to thank Harry and Harriet for thinking this meeting up, as it was their idea, and not mine. I am very proud of them both having this idea to highlight their plight and hopefully eventually educate the two leggers into stopping this atrocious and disgusting behaviour, discarding their unwanted food wrapping in the countryside and landscape in our towns and villages where we live. If we can make this happen it would be brilliant for everyone living on our planet. Now I will hand it over to you, Harriet and Harry."

Harriet says "Harry, you go first."

"OK," says Harry, "it has been so exciting to be allowed to stay up all day. Hello everyone, I am Harry the hedgehog and I am fed up with all of this rubbish sticking to my spikes. I'm walking around like a ball of rubbish, it's horrible, it gets around my feet and trips me up and when I try to pull it off it gets stuck in my teeth and in my mouth, nearly choking me. We need to act quickly now; we can do this together and make a difference. Harriet will now tell you what we think we can all do. Over to you, Harriet."

"Hi to all of you and thank you again for coming today and listening to myself and Harry's ideas. We had our own meeting the other day and decided how we and all the animals can make a difference. I will try to explain and outline our thoughts. We came up with the idea that cleaning up the woods/ forests/rivers/pathways ourselves – collecting all the rubbish we can find, and taking it to one place in the woods, maybe the hollow of a tree or a big hole, where it won't blow about and when we've got enough, we will have another meeting to implement our plan.

"Plan A: all of us find the paths the children use going to school with their parents and make barricades out of the rubbish, so they can't get past. We can do this at night when no one can see us. This way the children will get on to their parents and ask questions like 'what's happening here?'. I think the children are our best hope, because it's quite obvious that their parents aren't that bothered; you've all seen them throw their litter out of their car windows and not use litter bins, it's not the children's fault. The parents should know better and teach the children. We all know the children love animals, so let's get them on our side secretly, so their parents aren't aware, that's a start. Over to the circle now for questions and answers. What do you think?" At this point everyone stood up, clapping, stamping, barking, whistling, flapping their wings in appreciation for Harriet's speech.

Harry and Harriet sat down and waited for the applause to stop. Just as Harry was about to sit on his stone, Trap the mouse shouted, "Look out, you're about to sit on me."

Harry looked down, "I am sorry Trap, I didn't see you there. By the way, how did you get here? It's a long way to travel for a little mouse."

"Oh, that was easy, I got a lift on the back of Nutty the squirrel." "Yes, I thought I saw you," said Harry. "I thought Nutty had brought his packed lunch. I hope not," said Trap.

"Right, calm down everyone," said Twit, and let's hear what the rest of the animals have got to say. Right," said Twit. Bill the badger stood up first. "Yes Bill, what are your thoughts?" Bill was getting tired as he was ready for his daytime sleep.'

"I have watched these two leggers in their cars, eating things and then throwing their empty packets through the car windows, not looking where they are going and they drive too fast and sometimes they run over us. I hate them." "Well, I don't blame you," said Twit, "but that won't get us anywhere. We need to get through to them and get them on our side and maybe then they will realise and slow down as well. Good point, Bill.

"Next, Milly the mole, you can't have a problem, surely. You live underground."

"How do you know?" replied Milly, "you are lucky to live in a tree. I get about making tunnels, so I can travel unnoticed through the forest, but I do keep bumping into tin cans, glass bottles, some broken and sharp which have been trodden into the ground. I can't see them as I am blind but when I am digging, they cut my paws I have to find a way around them, it's so dangerous. This never used to happen."

"Great point Milly, thank you." Yes Maurice the cat, he has got his paw up "Sorry" said Twit, "but as I explained to Smelly I couldn't get to see everybody, anyway, thank you for coming, what have you got to say?"

"My name is Maurice. I am the cat who got my head stuck in the tin can. I tried to get it off but the more I struggled, the tighter it seemed to get. It was stuck on my head for days and I thought I was going to die, and I would have died if it hadn't been for the kindness of the two leggers Olly and Eddie that found me. It took them ages to get the tin can off my head. As they pulled, I thought my head was going to come off, it was very painful, Then they took me to a big old house near where they found me and they wrapped me in a blanket and put me in front of a massive log fire. Anyway, I am very lucky and pleased I am here to tell the tale, they aren't all bad, just some of them. Harriet's right, they need educating on the dangers to us and all wildlife allowing their rubbish to blow about. I would love to help."

"Good story Maurice, thank you. Yes Joe the crow, you go next, what have you got to say?"

"Well, I've got lots to say, some good some bad. I will start with the good. Where I live is near a lot of houses at the edge of the woods, the two leggers are good at putting out food for the birds  which is really tasty, and we get a varied diet too. Then we have the bad side; they throw out their burger boxes with half eaten burgers in them into the road where it is busy with traffic. Then the cars run over them. That's OK, because we can get at the burgers – but it's a risky job, trying to get your dinner and making sure you don't get run over at the same time. Then the empty box just blows away into the fields and countryside, littering everywhere. They need teaching they need to take their litter home to recycle it, we don't mind a bit of left-over burgers though."

"OK Joe, that was a long speech but a good one, thanks.

"Last one now," says Twit. "It is getting late and some of you have got a long way to get back home and some of you have missed out on your sleep today.

"Yes, Goofy the beaver you're next, you have been stood up for ages. Go ahead, what have you got to say?"

"My name is Goofy, I live down by the river and I make dams out of natural things like logs, twigs leaves and mud, so we can swim and also make our homes. These things were great until a few years ago, when plastic bottles, crisp packets, plastic boxes and all other types of plastic that floats, started to arrive. It creates a big problem. When we are trying to build our dams, it gets stuck between the branches, causing a temporary blockage. Then after all our hard work and we think the dam is finished the pressure of the water pops the bottles through the dam, followed by the crisp packets and the rest of the rubbish. The next thing, our dam collapses and all the plastic is washed down the river into the ocean where it creates havoc for the fish and sea creatures, it can also kill them, as well as us."

"Thanks, Goofy, that was really important to let us know your point of view on what's happening in our rivers as well as on land. Right," said Twit, "I would like to bring this meeting to a close and thank you all for turning up. I think this will be the first of many meetings. If we are going to get through to the two leggers we need to make them realise what they are doing to the environment which effects all of us.

"I think this is great of Harry and Harriet's to highlight the seriousness of this situation and the idea to create blockages by making dry dams across the footpaths leading to the schools in your area would be good too. Then the children will ask their parents and say, 'what is going on, why is the path blocked?'

"Brilliant," said Twit. "We will arrange in groups in the next few weeks go to Goofy the Beaver's house on the river and ask him to teach us how to build a dam on these school paths. We can work in the middle of the night when no one's around. All in favour shout 'Yes'." They all replied excitedly.

"I think we're onto something here," said Nutty, who hadn't spoken yet.

"I think you're right," said Twit.
"Please can I say something before we go," said Willy the Woodpecker.
"Yes," said Twit.
"I think it would be another extremely good idea if each one of us in the group going to build these dams, makes a mould next to the dam and put in our footprints. Then this will get through to let

them know who has done this and we are very serious. They will know that the animals in the woods are rebelling against pollution and are totally fed up with all the mess."

"A great idea," said Twit. "You will all be able to leave your individual signature for the children to look up and see who's been here in the night. Last thing I will fly around this week and visit you all and put you into teams and by then I will have a plan for you all…"

It had been a very long day and all the animals started to make their way home.

Bill the badger went back to his set for a nap so he could get ready for the evening, as badgers are nocturnal. Sly the fox also went to get himself ready for the evening's hunting. Joe the crow went high up in the trees to roost for the night. Snowy the rabbit went to join his family down in the burrow and Snid the grass snake slid under a large stone coiled himself around and settled down for the night.

Ben the sheepdog made his way back to Berristall Hall Farm for his tea before snuggling down in his kennel for the night. Willy the woodpecker tucked his head under his wing and went to sleep in a hole in the tree trunk. Goofy the beaver slipped away into the marshes and Rodney the water rat swam down the river to a safe shady bank. Loner the goose went back to the pond at the farm and Trap the mouse hitched a lift home on Nutty the squirrel's back. Spotty the deer travelled back to safety of the wood, while Jug the hare hid away in his form on the ground. Milly the mole had long gone far down under ground. Scratty the wood pigeon roosted high up in the tree for the night. Maurice the cat made his way through the village to his new home to join his friend Scrappy. Not forgetting Twit the owl as he flew around making sure everyone was safe before he landed in his tree for the evening watch.

Not far away under a large pile of dry leaves was Spike and the hedgehog family having a well-earned rest before a night's foraging. All the animals had a lot of work to do in the weeks to come. This is just the beginning of the rest of our lives. Let's hope by having this meeting and doing something together to try to change the two leggers way of thinking will help the next generation to make a better environment for the future of all of us.

It took the whole of the following week for Twit to fly around putting the animals in the appropriate groups so they could go out on a chosen night to do whatever they could do best using their unique inherited skills –

Bill the badger was teamed up first with Snowy the rabbit and Sly the fox. Bill and Snowy were used to digging holes so Twit gave them instructions for the footings to create a good foundation for the dams. Sly was put on the team to oversee the work was carried out – whilst his job was to be a night watch to guard Bill and Snowy, frightening away any unwanted guests that might me lurking around in the night. Not many animals would tackle Sly.

Twit then chose Goofy the beaver and Ben the

sheep dog. Their role was as follows: Goofy would nibble all the branches and twigs with his big teeth so they could be intermingled into the main barrier and woven into the dam-like structure. Ben's role was to pick up all the branches and twigs and take them to the trenches that Bill and Snowy had dug; he was used to fetching sticks when being trained as a sheep dog. Next it was Smelly the pig's turn. He was chosen for his ability to tread the mud into the trench where the twigs and branches have been placed, all making up the barricade so that they could start adding the plastic waste that they had all collected from the woods.

Next came the assistance of all the rest of the animals now the barrier was in place. They were all instructed to pick up whatever they could carry out from the pile of plastic waste and take it to the dams. Everyone joined in. Lona the goose picked bits of plastic up in her beak and with her long neck was able to press them into the middle of the twigs. Willy the woodpecker flew down and spiked different types of rubbish with his strong beak, with Joe the crow who carried the plastic waste. They both flew back to the dams and dropped them like delivering bombs and then went back for more. Jug the hare punched them into place and jumped on them to secure a good fixing in the dam. Snid the grass snake did whatever he could into weaving the plastics amongst the dam as he slipped and slithered

between the twigs. All the rest of the team helped in their own way and contributed brilliantly to making the dam impenetrable and blocking up the pathways that would stop the parents and children on their way to school. This would bring to their attention the plight of the waste plastics which are causing damage to our world.

They worked late into the night to block all access routes to the school. Then they all left their footprints in the carefully made mug patch which Smelly had prepared for them, so that the children and their parents could see straight away who was responsible for these obstructions which were made to alert the two leggers.

The next morning the parents arrive at the school gates and, to their astonishment, they saw all of what looked like a pile of rubbish. Leo and Molly's mum Carole Shouted; this is disgusting. Someone has been fly tipping.
"What's fly tipping, Mum?" asked Molly.
"Fly tipping is when people are too lazy to take their rubbish to the tip or recycling centres, they would rather dump it for someone else to sort out. It's so unfair."
Just at that point another mum called Paula steps forward and takes a closer look at what they were all thinking is a pile of rubbish. "This doesn't look like it's been dumped to me," she said. She calls to the other parents, "Come over here and take a

closer look everyone," so they all gathered round quite sheepishly and a bit wary of what has been going on.

Lauren, Billie's Mum says, "Look, don't step any further, there is some sort of mud plaque on the ground. How strange, it looks like animals' footprints. Can anyone recognise any of them?" Slowly the mums and children took a closer look. Carole's son Leo shouted excitedly, "I know what footprint that is, it's a badger, I am sure it is." Leo has always been interested in animals. "I know as I have seen a badger set in the woods where the badgers live."

"That one looks like a goose's webbed foot," said Molly. "I've seen that footprint before when I helped Mum, put the geese away for the night at the farm."

One by one they started to take more interest on what has been going on. Then Sarah, Leo's and Molly's gran, shouts, "That's enough, it's nearly nine o'clock we should all be at school by now and I have got to get to work. We need to move this rubbish out of our way. Push it over to the side and get into school."

"Slow down," said Lucy, Leo and Molly's auntie, "I think everyone needs to stand back and look at what is happening here. This is not just an ordinary pile of rubbish, look at the way these twigs, branches and even the mud, have all been laid, so carefully and all the animals' footprints. It's very strange, I think someone is trying to tell us something. We need

to take some photos of it and study it. We can ask around to see if anyone knows anything."

More and more people started to gather round. A man from the council turned up called David. He said, "It looks like a dam to me or some sort of barricade trying to get someone's attention, sending a message across perhaps. I have never seen anything like it before. I think you should call James from Chestnut Polymers they recycle plastic and they maybe able to recycle this lot." Then headmaster Mr Humphrys appeared. He called across to the crowd of now anxious parents, "We seem to have dams at every entrance. I have called the police, they are on their way. I am afraid everyone will have to go home until this matter is sorted."

It was the talk of the village that day; crowds of people turned up over the following weeks to see what had happened, it went viral on social media, even the photos got into all the local papers.

BUT

It WAS the children in the end that realised what the message was, and what the animals were trying to tell them.

Back in the woods, Mr and Mrs Spike and children Harry and Harriet felt proud of what they and all the animals had achieved that day.

AFTER

ALL! THIS

WAS...

The Animals' Environmental Protest

About The Author

Chesney Orme is from the village of Bollington in Cheshire and has lived there all his life. The motivation for him to write this story came from his lifelong passion and pioneering work in plastic recycling. In the early years of his involvement with plastic recycling there was only Industrial plastic waste arisings that were taken care of by the industry itself. Then came the advent of post-consumer plastic packaging which when discarded wilfully blights our countryside and the habitat for our wildlife to live in. Using his experience and knowledge of the various plastics which are used has pioneered a process to enable this type of material to be converted into useful end products, therefore creating a demand for this type of waste. Hopefully in the future these types of packaging materials will have an everlasting life, preserve our precious resources, and encourage people not to discard their packaging and think of the health and wellbeing of wildlife.

Lightning Source UK Ltd.
Milton Keynes UK
UKHW040924301122
413110UK00005B/94